UNIQUE AND UNSTOPPABLE:
MYA'S JOURNEY TO OVERCOMING A DISABILITY"

Written By: Ladi Miz

THIS BOOK BELONGS TO:

____

DEDICATION

I dedicate this book to my kids and my unborn grandkids.

once there was a little girl named Mya.

She really enjoyed playing with her friends however; she would feel like there was something that was different about her.

One day, she discovered that she had a disability that made it harder for her to do certain things.

School
School Bus

At first, Mya struggled to accept her disability.

She felt like she was different from the other kids and that she couldn't do the same things they could.

But as she began to explore her abilities more, she realized that she was just like everyone else.

She could run, jump, and play just as well as her friends.

HERO

She learned to embrace her disability and saw it as a unique part of who she was.

Mya realized that she was just as equal and capable as everyone else, and that her disability didn't define her

THE END

About the author:

Ladi Miz is a Mother, Wife, Entrepreneur, Songwriter, Community Advocate and Author.

POEM

Sometimes things can be hard to do
When our bodies don't work like others do
But just because we're a little different
Doesn't mean we can't be magnificent

We might need some help to get around
But that doesn't mean we're stuck on the ground
We can still run and jump and play
And have fun with our friends every day

We might have to try a little bit harder
But we can still be a superstar-er
We can do anything we set our minds to
And show the world what we can do

So let's embrace what makes us unique
And never let our disabilities make us weak
We're strong, we're brave, we're amazing too
And we can overcome anything we go through

POEM

In a world that moves so fast
It may take me longer
To grasp what's going on
 I often wonder how others around me seem so strong

I later realized I have what I need inside
I'm unquie so I stand tall with pride.
Sometimes I see things in a different way
Yes I'm different and that's Okay

I might not always know what to say
Or understand things right away
But I have a heart that's full of love
And that's something that shines above

I see the world in a unique way
And that's something that's here to stay
I might have autism, that's true
But it doesn't make me much different than you
I have great qualities I"m smart, funny, beautiful
And that's just to name a few

So remember autism is something I have, not something I am
In a world full of diamonds I am a gem
We're strong, we're brave, we're amazing too
And we can overcome anything we go through

NOTES

NOTES

NOTES

www.ingramcontent.com/pod-product-compliance
Lightning Source LLC
Chambersburg PA
CBHW042143030726

47599CB00002B/594